Newcastle

Lions

This book was generously donated to the
Newcastle Library by

Farrah Lovie

2nd

Gift-A-Book ~ 2021-2022

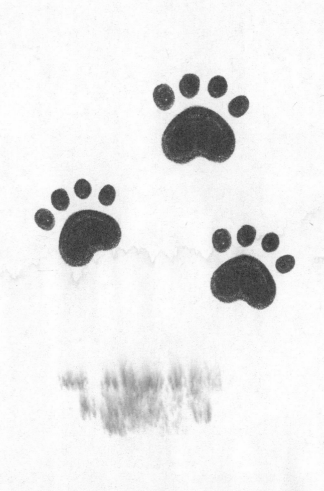

GOOD D🐾G
1

Home Is Where the Heart Is

by
Cam Higgins

Newcastle Elementary School
8400 136th Ave SE
Newcastle, WA 98059
425-837-5825

illustrated by
Ariel Landy

LITTLE SIMON

New York   London   Toronto   Sydney   New Delhi

LITTLE SIMON
An imprint of Simon & Schuster Children's Publishing Division
1230 Avenue of the Americas, New York, New York 10020
First Little Simon hardcover edition December 2020
Copyright © 2020 by Simon & Schuster, Inc.
Also available in a Little Simon paperback edition.
All rights reserved, including the right of reproduction in whole or in part in any form. LITTLE SIMON is a registered trademark of Simon & Schuster, Inc., and associated colophon is a trademark of Simon & Schuster, Inc.
For information about special discounts for bulk purchases, please contact Simon & Schuster Special Sales at 1-866-506-1949 or business@simonandschuster.com.
The Simon & Schuster Speakers Bureau can bring authors to your live event. For more information or to book an event contact the Simon & Schuster Speakers Bureau at 1-866-248-3049 or visit our website at www.simonspeakers.com.
Designed by Leslie Mechanic
Manufactured in the United States of America 0121 FFG
10 9 8 7 6 5 4 3 2
Library of Congress Cataloging-in-Publication Data
Names: Higgins, Cam, author. | Landy, Ariel, illustrator.
Title: Home is where the heart is / by Cam Higgins; illustrated by Ariel Landy.
Description: New York: Little Simon, 2020 | Series: Good dog; 1 |
Audience: Ages 5–9. | Audience: Grades K–1. | Summary: Rambunctious puppy Bo, who lives with his human family on a farm, loses his dog tag and enlists his barnyard animal friends to help him find it.
Identifiers: LCCN 2020045391 | ISBN 9781534479005 (paperback) | ISBN 9781534479012 (hardcover) | ISBN 9781534479029 (eBook)
Subjects: CYAC: Dogs—Fiction. | Animals—Infancy—Fiction. | Farm life—Fiction. | Domestic animals—Fiction. | Lost and found possessions—Fiction.
Classification: LCC PZ7.1.H54497 Ho 2020 | DDC [Fic]—dc23
LC record available at https://lccn.loc.gov/2020045391

CONTENTS

The Mud Bath

Mud.

Is there anything better than the cool feeling of it against your fur or the way it squishy-oozes between your paws?

And the smell! The sweet perfume of grass and springtime and earth. There is nothing like fresh mud.

Of course, I know I shouldn't have rolled around in mud, but that morning was special.

It had rained for the past three entire days on the Davis farm, which meant I was stuck in the house.

Being inside wasn't the worst thing in the world because I got to spend time with my human family.

Jennica and Darnell are my human mom and dad. They make great lap pillows, scratch behind my ears, and like to play fetch.

I've even trained them to give me leftovers when I've been good.

They say, "Good dog, Bo," because
that's my name, and then they scrape
yummy scraps into my food bowl.

I also have a human sister and brother, Imani and Wyatt. We are best friends, and we share everything!

Beds.

Socks.

Sticks.

Well, okay, maybe not sticks. I think sticks are the best.

What else is chewy on the inside and crunchy on the outside? I try to share them with Imani and Wyatt, but they keep throwing them away no matter how many times I bring them back.

Humans are funny like that.

Staying inside was fine when it rained for so long, but I'm more of an outside dog.

I like to spend my days exploring the farm and visiting my animal friends.

There's Star and Grey and their foal, Comet. She loves to chase me around. One day she might even catch me!

There's also a head hen named Clucks.

And there's a head
rooster named Rufus.
They're nice, even if
they peck at my feet
when I come near.

Nanny Sheep always reminds me
not to scare Clucks and Rufus. They
get jumpy around dogs, I guess.

And then there's Zonks. He's my pig pal.

Which brings me back to the mud. As soon as I saw the sunshine and clear skies that morning, I dashed out the front door before Imani and Wyatt could even put on their boots.

I went straight to the pigpen.

"Hi, Bo," Zonks oinked as he tumbled in the mud.

I stopped and admired the mess. "Wow! It's so . . . dirty!"

That made Zonks smile. "Some animals love rain because it brings rainbows, but not me. I love rain because it brings mud!"

"Can I try?" I asked.

Zonks plopped onto his back and waved with his hoof. "Come on in."

I stepped forward, and my paw sank into the gooey mud. I couldn't help myself. This was going to be fun.

I flopped onto my back and rolled all around. The mud covered my fur like a cool, soft blanket.

"Bo! Where are you, boy?" It was Imani calling me. I should have run to her, but I was in mud heaven.

13

Wyatt reached the pigpen first. He stared at me and shook his head.

Then Imani joined him at the fence and moaned, "Good grief, Bo!"

I gave a playful bark to invite them in.

But humans don't always understand Dog.

And from the looks on their faces, I don't think humans will *ever* understand mud.

Barn Cats

Here's a secret: I trust Imani and Wyatt.

They may not love mud as much as I do yet, but they know what's best for a pup like me.

So when they called me, I knew it was time to go.

I said goodbye to Zonks.

Then I said goodbye to the perfect, muddy pigpen and followed the kids back to the house.

Everyone could tell what was coming next. I was headed for the bath.

Baths aren't so bad. I don't mind them much. But there are some animals on the farm who do not like them at all.

Two of those animals are named King and Diva.

Imani and Wyatt call them barn cats, but I call them *trouble*.

Diva stood on the front porch and hissed when we walked up. "Bo, you poor thing. There's something stuck on your back!"

"What? Where?" I cried.

I wiggled this way and that, trying to see what it could be.

"Oh, Diva, don't you know?" King said with a smirk. "That's just the way dogs always look . . . covered in mud and completely clueless!"

See what I mean? Trouble.

Luckily Wyatt scooted those mean cats away. "Get, you two! You know the rules. Barn cats keep to the barn."

Then he went to run my bath as Imani plopped me down. We sat together on the porch.

"You sure love mud, Bo, don't you?" she asked, scratching behind my ear.

I wagged my tail, and some mud shook loose.

I could hear Diva hiss again in the distance, but Imani just giggled. She has the best giggles!

Hearing her laugh is maybe even better than rolling in mud. *Maybe.*

When the bath was ready, Imani picked me up and brought me inside. She didn't want me to track dirt on the floor.

I thought I was getting too big to be carried, but it felt really nice to be in her arms. Almost as good as mud.

3

Lost Tag

Imani set me down in the bathroom. The tile floor was cold and made me shiver a little.

"Did you check the water to make sure it isn't too hot?" Imani asked Wyatt.

"Yes, Imani," Wyatt said. "I know how to make a bath for Bo."

I peeked into the tub. There were lots of bubbles and nice smells in the water. It wasn't too deep. Wyatt really does know how to make a nice bath.

He took off my bandanna and my collar, and then I climbed into the tub. I took care not to splash.

The water was warm and nice, and
it felt so good. I lay down on my belly
so I wouldn't slip.

Wyatt stroked my head and held me gently. Imani reached for the showerhead, turned it on, and let the water fall over me like a soft rain. I closed my eyes and kept still.

"Good boy, Bo," Imani said.

She wet my back and my tail and my tummy. Then Imani and Wyatt rubbed shampoo all over my fur.

I was in doggy heaven!
Even the sudsy
squish sounds
made me
smile, until I
tasted some of
the soap and
yuck!

"Oops, almost over, Bo," said Wyatt as he wiped the bubbles away from my mouth.

When we were done, Imani pulled the drain plug.

I watched the water rush down in a swirl.

Then Imani rinsed me off with the
showerhead again.

As the suds ran off
my fur, I was a little
bit sad to see the mud
wash away. But I
wasn't too sad. There
would be more mud
another day.

There is *always* more mud on the farm. We practically grow mud here!

I was squeaky clean now, so Wyatt lifted me out of the tub, and Imani wrapped me in a fluffy blue towel.

Towels are soft and cozy, but they don't always get a pup dry. Imani and Wyatt take such good care of me. The least I could do was help them get the job done.

I *shook shook shook* my whole body, and a spray of water flew in every direction.

Imani and Wyatt squealed and laughed.

Then I ran! The wind would dry me. I darted into Wyatt's bedroom and rolled around on the carpet.

Then I dashed into Imani's room and rolled on her rug.

If you have never rubbed your ears and nose and back on a carpet, you do not know what you are missing. It feels *so* scratchy and good!

A few more shakes and a few more rub-rolls on the ground, and I was good as new, dry as a bone.

Oooh, bones. Yum!

When Wyatt and Imani found me, they were still giggling. I wagged my tail and ran to them.

"You're lucky you're so cute," Imani
told me.

She was right. I sure am a lucky
pup. And I'm pretty cute . . . if I do say
so myself.

Wyatt bent to put my collar on.
As he fastened it around my neck,
he said, "Huh, your tag is missing."

My tag was *missing*? Oh boy, this sounded like a Bo Davis mystery that needed to be solved!

Ultra–Doggy–Alarm

Wyatt might not be very worried about my missing tag, but I sure was.

There was a time, long ago, when I didn't have a tag of my own.

I don't remember much about the pound, but I remember when the Davis family found me. Imani and Wyatt were much smaller . . . and so was I!

Then they adopted me and brought me home.

They also gave me my special tag. It was shaped like a heart and had my name on one side and my address and phone number on the other. It's supposed to help me if I ever get lost. Luckily, I haven't had to use it.

But I love my tag. It reminds me that I'm part of the Davis family. So if it was missing, I *had* to find it.

The first thing I needed to do was get outside.

Every dog knows the secret to getting outdoors—it's easy.

All you have to do is act like you have to go to the bathroom. It works every time.

You start by standing at the door and scraping your paw on it. Then you look back at your humans.

If that doesn't work, you go over to
your people, put your paw on them,
and whimper just a little. You have
to be careful with the whimpering,
though. If you cry too much, your
people might think you're hurt or sick
and take you to the vet.

If that doesn't work, then it's time to bark your head off and really scratch at the door. Running in circles helps too. I call this move the ultra-doggy-alarm. It's very powerful, so I try to be responsible and save it for when nothing else works.

That morning I only needed to wait by the door, and Wyatt came. But before he let me out, he made me promise not to go back in the mud and get dirty again.

I licked his hand to show I understood. I'd try my very best to stay clean.

The first place I raced to was Zonks's pen.

"Hi, Zonks," I said.

"Hello, Bo," Zonks said. He was still lounging in the mud. Oh, it looked so nice. But no, I reminded myself: I had a mission. There was no time for mud.

"Have you seen my tag?" I asked. "It fell off my collar."

"Well, there was something shiny in the mud," said Zonks. "One of the chicks came by and took it. You know how those chicks love shiny objects."

Oh no, not chickens. Why did it have to be chickens?

5

A Game of Chicken

Don't get me wrong. Chickens are nice, but I did *not* want to bother the chickens if I didn't have to.

Imani says chickens are just jumpy creatures. I say they're scared of everything.

And the problem is, when they are scared, they are super loud.

Maybe I could sneak into the chicken coop, find my tag, and sneak out without being seen.

I tiptoed quietly over to their pen. Most of the chickens were outside, walking along the far edge of the grass and pecking at the ground.

When it rains, we get more than mud on the farm. The rain also brings out worms.

Chickens *love* worms. In fact, worms might be a chicken's most favorite snack.

So while the flock was hunting for squiggly food, I saw my chance.

I slipped under the fence and into their coop. I saw nests, and inside the nests were eggs. But I did not see my shiny tag.

It was time to get out of there before I was discovered.

I turned to leave when I heard something behind me.

"Hello? *Cluck, cluck.* What are you doing in here? *Cluck, cluck!*"

It was Clucks, the head hen. She's the boss of all the chickens, which means she was also the loudest.

Remember the ultra-doggy-alarm? *Everything* sets off the ultra-*chicky*-alarm for Clucks.

Before I could explain, Clucks began to *bawk* and screech. She flapped her wings and chased me right out of the coop.

But all the other chickens were there in the yard, waiting for me. I was surrounded!

They began clucking and flapping their wings. I might have thought the sky was falling, they were acting so scared.

Suddenly Clucks and Rufus, the head rooster, stepped out of the coop together. The other chickens quieted down.

"*Cluck*. What is the meaning of this, Bo? Why were you in our coop?" Clucks said.

"I'm sorry. I lost my shiny tag this morning when I was visiting Zonks," I explained. "He told me one of your chicks found it."

Rufus waved a wing at the chicks and nodded to them. Rufus doesn't speak much—just when he wakes us up with the sunrise every morning.

A fluffy yellow chick stepped forward and said, "*Cheep, cheep.* I found a shiny thing. I was looking for worms near Zonks's mud, and I saw it. So I was picking it up when Nanny Sheep stopped me. She said the shiny thing did not belong to me."

"*Cluck*, and what did you say to Nanny Sheep?" Clucks asked.

The little chick looked nervous. "Um, I said, 'Finders keepers, I have sharp peepers!' *Cheep*."

The chickens all ruffled their wings and clucked quietly. The other chicks' eyes grew larger than skillets!

Everyone knew Nanny Sheep was the kindest animal on the farm. Only a silly little chick would speak to her so rudely.

"I hope you apologized right away," said Clucks.

All eyes were on the chick.

He looked very ashamed. "I told Nanny Sheep I was sorry. Then I gave her the shiny thing. That's where it is now. I promise! *Cheep!*"

Wow! I was *good* at solving mysteries! I was lucky, too. I'd get to see Nanny Sheep *and* get my tag back.

6

Counting Sheep

Nanny Sheep lived in the field with the other sheep.

Sometimes the cows came out to graze. Now and then the horses came outside to run and munch on hay also. But everyone else must have stayed in the barn, because today I only saw sheep.

I love the sheep. They look like tiny clouds, and their soft wool feels like pillows. But take my word for it: *never* try to nap on them.

Actually, that's how I first met Nanny Sheep.

I was playing fetch in the field and I'd gotten so tired from running, I could hardly keep my eyes open.

So when I found a bale of hay
with a mound of the softest, fluffiest
cloud piled in front of it, I couldn't
help myself. I hopped up onto the
hay and leaped into the middle of
that cloud.

But the cloud was not as soft as it
looked. And it was angry.

In fact, it wasn't a cloud at all. It
was a flock of sheep taking a nap.
When I landed on top of them, they
sprang up and ran away. I fell to the
ground.

Sheep do not like being jumped on.
They don't like it one bit.

I told them that I was sorry and explained that I'd thought they were a cloud. That just made the sheep laugh at me.

Nanny Sheep didn't laugh, though.

Instead, she shushed the sheep and made the kindest announcement I had ever heard.

"One day this puppy will grow up to be a big dog, and he will herd us and help the farmers take care of us," Nanny Sheep said. "We should all be friends, and friends do not laugh at each other."

The other sheep stopped laughing, but I started to giggle. I couldn't help it!

"I'm sorry," I woofed. "But actually, it *is* pretty silly that I thought you were a cloud!"

Then everyone laughed again, even Nanny Sheep. The sheep and I have been good friends ever since.

Now I found Nanny Sheep resting in the shade beneath a tree.

"Hello, Bo," she said. "Are you finally here to herd the flock?"

"No, Nanny Sheep, not yet," I said. "I'm looking for something you took from a chick. It's a shiny thing. Do you know it?"

"Oh, yes, I do know it," Nanny Sheep replied. "But I'm afraid I do not have it. It belonged to Blue, and I gave it back to him."

Nanny Sheep looked up and called to Blue. The blue jay flew down from his nest high in the tree and landed next to us.

"Could you tell Bo about your shiny object?" Nanny Sheep asked him.

"The shiny thing you found for me?" Blue said. "It's a small bracelet that the girl gave me. She no longer plays with it."

I sighed.

Blue was telling the truth. Imani loved birds, and she sometimes left tiny toys for Blue on her windowsill.

Blue had lost the bracelet in the rain, but Nanny Sheep returned it.

Well, the mystery of the muddy, shiny thing was solved. But the mystery of my lost tag was not!

Scrapper

On the way back to my house, I heard someone in the woods.

"*Bark*-hey! *Bark*-Bo?"

It was Scrapper, my best dog buddy. He lived next door with the Bryson family.

Scrapper is a small pup, like I am, but his fur is shorter and yellow.

He has a thinner tail that wags when he's happy, and he was born with three legs. Other than that, we are exactly alike!

Scrapper was so muddy, he was covered from head to tail! He jumped up and down and ran in circles as I trotted over to him.

"Isn't this mud great?" Scrapper cheered. "I've been rolling in it all day! It feels so good. I even have mud in my ears. Oh, hey, wait a minute."

Scrapper stopped and stared at me. He walked right up to me and sniffed the air.

"Why aren't you muddy, buddy? And why do you smell like flowers? Did you—*GASP*—take a bath?"

"Yeah, but I played in the mud this morning," I said. "Now I'm looking for something. Something really important."

"Oh! Oh! Oh! Are you looking for buried treasure?" he asked.

I woofed *no*.

"Oh! Oh! Oh! Are you looking for more mud?" he asked.

I shook my head.

"Wait! Are you looking for the monster in the woods?" he asked as he shook off all the mud.

I answered no again, but I should tell you about Scrapper and the monster. He believed there was a monster living in the forest.

He swore he saw it once, and now
he always hunts for it.

"No, I'm looking for my tag," I said.

Scrapper gave a big laugh. "That's
no big deal. I lose my tag all the time.
Just retrace your steps and check the
places you went today."

I lowered my tail. "I already did that and still didn't find it."

"I bet you lost it at the house," Scrapper suggested. "You can look for it after we find the monster!"

Again with the monster!

"Could we do that another time?" I asked. "I really want to find my tag. It means a lot to me."

"Of course!" Scrapper wagged his tail. "Good luck!"

I wished Scrapper good luck with his monster too. I'm sure he'll find it one of these days.

8

King and Diva

I walked back to the house and saw King and Diva waiting for me on the porch. They were always waiting for me on the porch.

"Stop! Who goes there?" King hissed.

"You know who it is," I said. "It's me, Bo. I live here, remember?"

"Hmmm," purred Diva. "That rings a bell. But the Bo who lives here has a tag with his name on it."

King and Diva slunk down the steps and stopped in front of me.

"And I don't see a tag on your collar," said Diva. "Maybe we should keep you out?"

I laughed nervously and tried to move past them. But the cats flicked their tails in my face and blocked the way to the porch.

"This isn't funny. You'd better let me pass," I said, "or—or I'll start barking!"

"Oh no! Not *barking*!" King and Diva pretended to be scared. "Oh, *please* don't bark! Whatever will we do? We're helpless against loud puppies who bark!"

They hissed and meowed a mean laugh.

"Come on, cats. Let me by. I need to find my tag," I said.

"Oh, right. Your tag," King said as he showed off his sharp teeth. "I heard something about your missing tag. What was it? I know! I heard it was all the way in the *up*-upstairs."

"Really?" I tried to keep my tail from wagging, but I couldn't help it. I was too excited. Dogs are not very good at hiding their feelings, and I may be the worst at it.

Still, the up-upstairs was a strange place for my tag to be.

"You aren't trying to fool me, are you?" I asked the barn cats, even though I kind of knew the answer.

"Oh, Bo," Diva said with a grin. "Why would we ever do that?"

9

The Up—Upstairs

The up-upstairs was what Imani and Wyatt called the attic. It's where the family keeps all their extra stuff, like clothes and chairs and decorations, and even beds.

We animals stay away from the up-upstairs. It's scary. But if my tag was up there, I had to be brave.

I climbed up to the porch, nudged the screen door open with my nose, and went inside.

After I bounded up to the second floor, I ran to the up-upstairs door at the end of the hallway.

It never closed all the way. Wyatt said that's because our house was so old.

I opened the door easily with my paw. It was dark, and the darkness surprised me because it was still day outside. Maybe light didn't exist in the up-upstairs?

With a gulp, I started up the steps.

They creaked slowly with my every move. It sounded like someone was following me . . . or *something*.

Suddenly I really hoped that Scrapper had caught his monster today and that it wasn't right behind me.

Just in case, I scrambled up the stairs and bumped right into a box full of winter clothes.

Then I whirled around to see if the monster was behind me. No one was there.

I took a deep breath and looked around the room. Even though the sun shone outside, the up-upstairs was cast in shadows. Most of the windows were blocked by stuff.

I could only make out the hulking shapes of boxes and old furniture. It was going to be impossible to find my tag in here . . . even if the barn cats were telling the truth.

I was about to give up when a small
voice asked, "Can I help you?"

I tiptoed back toward the corner
with my tail tucked under my tummy.
I am not afraid to say that I am not a
brave pup.

"Are you, um, the monster in
the forest?" I forced myself to ask.

"Or are you a ghost that lives in the up-upstairs? Because if you are either of those things, I would like to leave."

"Don't be scared," said the voice. "I only want to help. We don't see many puppies up here."

"Well, I don't see many ghosts down there!" I whimpered.

"Ghosts? We aren't ghosts," the voice said. "We are spiders! Look up!"

I tipped my head back, and there was a spider, dangling from a thread just above me. It took every bit of courage not to run away.

"I—I'm Bo Davis," I said, "and I'm looking for my tag. See, it goes on my collar. It's shiny and heart-shaped. Have you seen it?"

The spider shook his tiny head. "I have not. But we will look for it."

I watched as more spiders hanging
from webs all over the ceiling flicked
their eyes around the room, searching.
Spiders have more eyes than me. That
was a lot of eyes looking for my tag.

"We do not see it here, I'm afraid,"
the spider said finally. "But let us send

a message to the other spiders in the house. Maybe they have seen it."

The spiders began to pluck at their webs, and I pricked my ears to listen. I could hear the quietest whisper of spider song. It sounded like a gentle breeze.

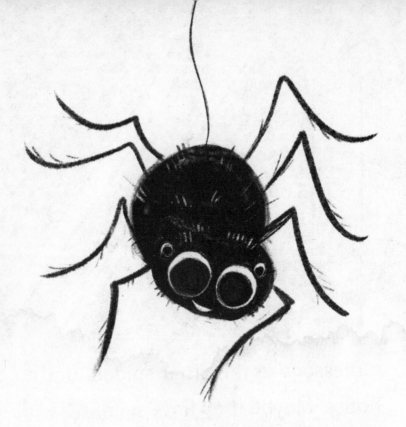

Then the spider above me smiled.
"We have found it downstairs, near
the bathroom!"

"Oh, wow, thank you, spiders!" I
said. "Thank you so much!"

I turned and bounded down the steps. My heart was pounding. I was so happy. Not only was my tag found but I had also made new friends! Plus, I had not met a monster or a ghost. That's good news for a pup like me!

Home Is Where the Heart Is

I raced down the hall and slid right into the laundry hamper by the bathroom. I wish I could tell you this was the first time that had happened. But it wasn't. Somehow I slip and bump into things a lot.

The laundry basket tipped over, and a towel fell on the floor.

It was my towel from this morning!
I sniffed it and could still smell the
shampoo and mud. Those are two
smells that go great together . . .
especially if you are a dog!

Wyatt and Imani heard the crash
and came running over.

"Oh, Bo, did you get muddy again?"
Wyatt asked.

I barked and rolled around on the
towel.

"No, he's clean as a whistle," said
Imani. "He seems to love that towel,
though."

Yes! The towel! Imani tried to pick it up, but I stepped on it with my paw.

"No, Bo. It's not playtime," she said. "And our towels are not toys."

Oh, sometimes I wish I could speak Human! It would make everyone's life so much easier!

Instead of shouting, *Hey, I think there's something UNDER the towel*, I got on my belly and rested my head on the towel. Then I gave Wyatt and Imani my biggest puppy dog eyes.

Wyatt bent down and picked up the towel. Something shiny fell out of the folds and bounced on the floor.

"Well, would you look at that!" Wyatt cheered. "You found your tag, Bo! Good dog!"

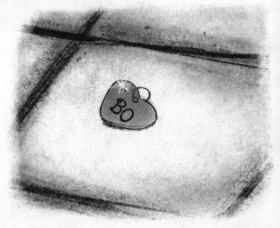

116

Wyatt slipped it back onto my collar while Imani found a tool to clamp its metal loop shut.

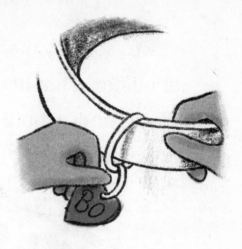

"There," she said, closing it. "Good as new. This tag should never fall off again."

With the mystery solved, we all went downstairs, where the kids poured some kibble into my bowl. Yum!

I was so busy that I had forgotten to eat all day. That had never happened before and would probably never happen again!

When I finished, I joined Wyatt and Imani on the sofa. They were reading books. I wished I could read books. It looked fun. But I wasn't going to learn that day.

I was dog-tired, which is like being a tired human times one hundred.

So I laid my head down on Imani's soft lap and closed my eyes. I'd had so many adventures, I think I earned a puppy nap. Besides, who knew what adventures awaited me tomorrow!

Here's a peek at Bo's next big adventure!

GOOD D🐾G ②

Raised in a Barn

The sky was a clear blue. Puffs of fluffy white clouds drifted above the Davis farm. The sunshine made the fur on my back feel nice and warm. Even the dirt smelled yummy, like leaves, flowers, and mud. I dug my paws deeper into the ground.

An excerpt from *Raised in a Barn*

It was the perfect day for a race!

Comet came bounding out of the barn. Her horse legs still seemed a little bit too long for her horse body as she trotted over to me.

Comet is the new horse. She is Star and Grey's foal, and she thinks she's fast.

But I'm Bo Davis! Everyone knows I am the fastest animal around.

I can run faster than a chicken. I can run faster than a sheep. I can even run faster than my human brother and sister, Wyatt and Imani.

Plus, I can almost outrun the family

truck, if it weren't for the fence I'm not supposed to cross.

That's why Comet and I needed to race: to prove once and for all who's the fastest on the Davis farm.

I greeted the young horse with a nod. "Morning, Comet."

"Hiya, Bo," she neighed cheerfully. "What a nice, sunny day!"

"It sure is," I said. "Are you ready to run?"

"You bet I am! And I'm going to win, too!" Comet said.

I woofed with a big puppy dog grin.

An excerpt from *Raised in a Barn*